P9-CRA-700

ARCHIE

First published in Great Britain in June 2012 by Bloomsbury Publishing Plc
Published in the United States of America in October 2012
by Bloomsbury Books for Young Readers
www.bloomsburykids.com

For information about permission to reproduce selections from this book, write to Permissions, Bloomsbury BFYR, 175 Fifth Avenue, New York, New York 10010

Library of Congress Cataloging-in-Publication Data
available upon request
ISBN 978-1-59990-936-3 (hardcover) • ISBN 978-1-59990-947-9 (reinforced)

Art created with mixed media
Hand lettering created by Domenica More Gordon

Printed in Belgium by Proost, Turnhout
2 4 6 8 10 9 7 5 3 1 (hardcover)
2 4 6 8 10 9 7 5 3 1 (reinforced)

Domenica More Gordon

NEW YORK LONDON NEW DELHI SYDNEY

RING
RING

FROM
GREAT
AUNT
BETTY

Hmmmm.....

SNIP
SNIP
SNIP

zzzzzz

pom pom pm de pom...

ohhh

WHIRR
WHIRR
WHIRR

oooh
oooh
woof
woof
woof
woof

RING
RING
RING

RING
RING
RING
RING
RING
RING
RING
RING
RING
RING

SNIP
SNIP
SNIP
SNIP

whirr
whirr
WHRR

woof
woof
woof
ohh
oohh
ooohh
WOOF
WOOF
woof woof

woof
woof
woof

woof
woof
woof
yip yip

ZZZZZZZ

RING
RING

TWEED
TAILOR-ING MADE EASY

hmmmmm

whirr
whirr
whirrrr
whir

GASP

Bow wow

WOW

RIN
RIN
RING
RING
RING
RIN
RING

RING
RING
RING
RING
RING
RING
RING

CLAP
WOOOOOOW
CLAP
CLAP

CLAP
CLAP
CLAP
YIP YIP
HOORAY

RING
RING
GREECE

zzzzzz

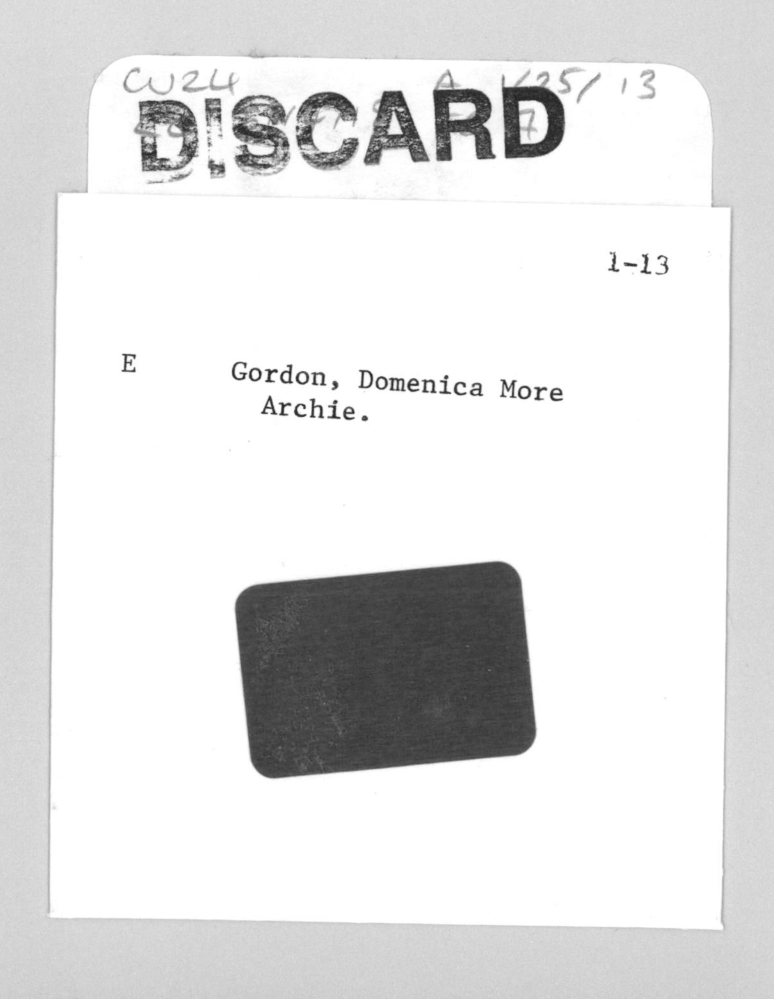
DISCARD
1-13
E
Gordon, Domenica More
Archie.